PRINCESSES DON'T FART
(THEY FLUFF)

ISBN 9798756244830

WRITTEN AND ILLUSTRATED BY
JANE BEXLEY

Princesses are fancy.
Princesses are polite.
Princesses are proper.
Princesses do **NOT** fart.

Of course, princesses have
gas just like everyone else.
But they know how to toot
in the most fancy, polite,
and proper ways!

Flutter Fluffs

A flutter fluff is a cute little toot with just enough wind to make a skirt flutter. Thankfully, these little toots don't smell so they are pretty safe to let loose.

Skirt Burst

Too many flutter fluffs can be a big problem. If too much gas gets trapped under her dress, a princess might have a skirt burst!

Tea Party Puffers

Princesses must outsmart their farts in fancy situations. Tea party puffers are quiet, tiny toots leaked out a little at a time instead of in one big, loud blow.

PUFF... PUFF... PUFF...

Fumigator

Princesses save their bigger toots for outside. A stroll through the garden is a great time to blow a big, stinky fumigator because the pretty scent of flowers can help hide the yucky smell.

Throne Thunder

Farting while sitting on a chair can be very loud. A princess only rips throne thunder when everyone else is distracted by a noisy performance.

Curtsey Creeper

Sometimes princesses are nervous and gassy when they meet new people. Thankfully, they can let out a curtsey creeper with an extra swish of their skirt to blow the stink away!

WOOSH!

Gas Slipper

Sometimes toots slip out no matter what you do. Just bending over to fix her shoe can launch a gas slipper if a princess isn't careful.

CRACK!

Windy Whistles

Not all toots need to be hidden. Some are actually useful! Princesses blow windy whistles to help them gracefully glide across the ice.

FSSSSSSSSS...

Pony Poppers

Bouncing on horseback rumbles up a lot of tummy bubbles. Princesses (and their horses) use those bubbles to blast pony poppers when they need a little boost.

Dragon Slayer

A princess's biggest, stinkiest, and most useful toot is the dragon slayer. This booty burp really comes in handy when it's time to save the day!

Royal Ripper

Sometimes toots are extra useful when a princess wants to have fun. A royal ripper is a big, ripe cheek flapper saved up for the perfect moment, like a friendly carriage ride.

Twinkle Toots

Dance class is another great place to let it rip. Synchronized twinkle toots make class fun for everyone! Well, almost everyone.

Bath Bombs

Outsmarting farts is exhausting. A relaxing bubble bath is the perfect place for a princess to drop some bath bombs at the end of the day.

Princesses are fancy.
Princesses are polite.
Princesses are proper.
Princesses do **NOT** fart...

...they fluff, puff, fumigate,
thunder, creep, slip, whistle,
pop, slay, rip, twinkle and
bomb... in the fanciest ways
possible, of course!

Made in United States
Troutdale, OR
11/05/2024